Muddy Four Paws

Jilly turned to take one last look as we left the yard (I was too much of a coward). She reported that Mud was standing in his kennel, pressed against the chicken wire, "Gazing after us."

"He trusted us," I said, "and we've betrayed him!"

"It wasn't our fault," said Jilly.

"He couldn't know that!"

"No, I know," said Jilly, and she took out her handkerchief, which was already crumpled into a wet ball, and wiped her eyes. "But we're doing what we can!"

Also available in the We Love Animals series:

Muddy Four Paws

Jean Ure

First published in Great Britain in 1998 by Scholastic Children's
Books, Commonwealth House, 1–19 New Oxford Street, London
WC1A 1NU, UK
A division of Scholastic Ltd

All inquiries should be addressed to:
Barron's Educational Series, Inc.
250 Wireless Boulevard
Hauppauge, NY 11788
http://www.barronseduc.com

International Standard Book No. 0-7641-0968-5

Library of Congress Catalog Card No. 98-48463

Library of Congress Cataloging-in-Publication Data
Ure, Jean.
        Muddy Four Paws / Jean Ure
                p.   cm. — (We love animals)
        Summary: Eleven-year-old Clara and her best friend
        rescue a huge and unruly abandoned dog, but her mother
        won't let Clara keep it until she finds out that the dog has
        something in common with Clara's younger brother Benjy.
                ISBN 0-7641-0968-5 (pbk.)
        [1. Dogs—Fiction. 2. Deaf—Fiction. 3. Physically
        handicapped—Fiction. 4. England—Fiction.] I. Title. II.
        Series: Ure, Jean. We love animals.
        PZ7.U64Mu   1999   98-48463
        [Fic] —dc21   CIP
                                                            AC

Printed in the United States of America
987654321

Chapter 1

I expect you've heard of Goody Two Shoes. Well, this is the story of a dog called Muddy Four Paws. A dog who changed my life *completely*. And my best friend, Jilly's, as well.

If Mud hadn't come into our lives, we would probably still be just two ordinary dippy 11-year-olds swooning over rock stars and giggling at childish jokes, not caring about the things that are going on all around us. Actually, I have to admit we still do a bit of swooning and giggling. Miss Milsom, at school, even has to separate us sometimes on account of our giggling so much. But when it comes to animals, we are both *deadly serious.*

And it is all because of Mud. It was Mud that brought about the great change in our lives.

As a matter of fact, it was the second great change that had happened to me. The first great change was when Mom and Dad split up and we sold our house in New York and moved to England to live in the countryside. That's where Mom was born. Not the wild, way-out sort of country; more what Mom calls "civilized country," which means you can still get to the supermarket to do your shopping, and go into town once a week (if you want to) to change your library books and drink coffee. But it also means that there are woods and fields instead of shops and office buildings, and country lanes that wind like snakes between the hedges instead of big dirty highways filled with traffic.

I thought at first I'd never get used to it. I thought it was too slow; that nothing ever happened. And I tell you, I nearly freaked when I saw the school I was to go to. A huge, enormous school with about a thousand kids!

Quite honestly, I felt like running away. I seriously considered it. The only thing that stopped me was not having any money. I told Mom that life was the pits and that I wished I'd never been born, and she said that she sometimes wished I'd never been born as well. And then she cried and said she didn't mean it, which actually I knew without her telling me, because my mom is cool and puts up with *a lot*. So we kissed and made up, and I promised that I would try really, really hard to adapt myself to this new way of life, while inside myself being utterly convinced that I never would.

Which just shows how wrong you can be, because shortly after that I met Jilly, who lives next door and is the same age as I am, and we discovered that we had simply tons in common, such as both being from one-parent families and both having lived in cities (Jilly was from London) and from that point on I began to think that life in England might not be so bad after all.

And then, of course, we found Mud, and nothing has ever been quite the same since. I wouldn't go back and live in the city now if you paid me a million dollars!

It makes me get goose pimples all over to think that, if Jilly and I hadn't come along when we did, poor Mud would have died the most terrible death.

We'd gone out on our bikes together, one Sunday morning, and were pedaling quite slowly and peaceably along Feather Down Lane, which leads to Feather Down, where in the summer, according to Jilly, there is a huge, stupendous fair with games, greased poles, and roller coasters. I am really looking forward to it!

Anyway, Jilly and I were just strolling along, minding our own business in the autumn sunshine, and discussing the sort of things that we liked to discuss. Boys, for instance. We talked about boys quite a lot last autumn. Now we tend to talk mostly about animals. Boys have faded into relative insignificance in our lives. ("And a good thing, too!" says Mom. She thinks 11 is *too young*.)

I remember that day, the day that Mud came into our lives, we were talking about this gorgeous hunk named Erik who was in the twelfth grade at Riddlestone High (the school that I made such a fuss about having to go to). The gorgeous thing about Erik was not only that he was gorgeous, but that he was lead guitar in a band called Troy that did gigs for school dances. Jilly and I were crazy about Erik! We were quite seriously discussing whether we should start up a fan club.

"Then we could get signed photographs," I said.

It was the signed photographs we were really after, but as it turned out, we never got around to starting the fan club because from that point on we thought about nothing except *animals.*

What happened was we rounded a bend in the lane and saw this car ahead of us. I guess about a hundred yards away, though I am not very good at distances. I would make a terrible witness. I couldn't even tell you what make of car it was, or its license plate number. Neither could Jilly, though she thinks it might perhaps have been a Ford. Or possibly something Japanese, like a Toyota, or something. In other words, she doesn't have any more idea than I do. But she is sure there was a nine somewhere in the number.

Huh! Big help that is.

All I personally can remember is that it was brown and it was a hatchback and it had pulled in to the side of the lane. The back was open, and as we cycled toward it we saw this man yank something out, something quite heavy, a box it looked like, and hurl it into the bushes. He then slammed down the hatchback, jumped into the driver's seat, and sped away at about 100 miles per hour in a cloud of dust.

"Creep!" yelled Jilly. And then she said to me, "We should have gotten the license plate number! Did you get the license plate number?"

I said, "No. Why?"

"Because he was *dumping*," said Jilly, "and dumping is against the law. People can get arrested for it. Cluttering up the countryside with all their rotten trash!"

I hadn't lived in the country long enough at this stage to realize that this was what people did. I knew that in New York you found mess all over the place, but I was still innocent enough to believe that the English countryside was clean and wholesome. (Apart from cow chips and horse droppings, but these are natural and you soon get used to them.)

Pedaling furiously, Jilly told me that Feather Down Woods were a favorite dumping ground. She said that wherever you went you found builders' rubble and old beds, and even coolers that people had chucked out of their cars.

"It's so *disgusting*. Look at it!"

Jilly had screeched to a halt and was pointing with a quivering finger where the man in the Ford (or the Toyota) had dumped his trash. I scuffed my foot along the ground and wheeled in beside her.

"Ugh!" I said. "That's foul!"

There were a load of old bricks and chunks of plaster, which obviously had been there some time because grass and purple weedy things were starting to grow over them. There was something that looked as if it was part of a car engine. There was an old TV set, with the screen bashed in. And there was a suitcase.

"That's what he chucked," said Jilly.

We both stood there, staring at it. It lay where it had fallen, part of it on dry land, part in a ditch full of revolting black gunk. It was quite a large suitcase, the kind that people roll on wheels.

"Wonder what's in it?" I said.

"Nothing valuable," said Jilly, "or the slime wouldn't have gotten rid of it."

Slime is short for slimeball. We are always calling people slimeballs. It's one of our words.

"Could be stolen money," I said.

"Why would he throw stolen money away?"

"Because he got scared, maybe."

We went on staring at the suitcase.

"Could be a body," I said.

"In a suitcase?"

"That's what they put them in."

"A body wouldn't fit into a suitcase!"

"It would if it was chopped up."

"Oh, stop it!" cried Jilly.

She is so much more squeamish than I am. I, for instance, adore horror movies and books that make you scared to go to bed. Jilly, in some ways, in spite of calling people creeps and slimeballs, is quite a wimp. She is also very blonde and bubbly and rather prettyish, whereas I am dark and rather plain; at any rate, not pretty, anyway. But I am not a wimp!

"I'm going to open it," I said.

"No! Don't!" Jilly grabbed at me. "It could

be a bomb!"

At that moment the suitcase moved. We both jumped back, Jilly with a strangled shriek. Even I made a small sort of noise that sounded something like "Eeurgh!" It is quite upsetting when a suitcase suddenly moves all by itself.

What it did was it tumbled down into the ditch, into all the stinky black gunk. And as it tumbled this sound came from it: a sound like a yelp and a bark and a whimper all rolled into one.

"It's a dog!" I cried.

I flung myself off my bike and rushed forward, but Jilly yelled at me to come back.

"Don't touch it!"

"But there's a dog in there! It could suffocate! It could *drown*!"

Jilly still didn't want me to go near it. She said that what we should do, we should ride off as fast as we could to the nearest house and get help. She said that a strange dog, especially one that had been cruelly shut up in a suitcase, could be dangerous.

"It could attack you. It could be a Rottweiler."

But I didn't think you could get a Rottweiler into a suitcase that size, and I didn't care if the dog did attack me. I couldn't just stand there and let it drown.

I said, "You wouldn't go off and leave it if it were a baby, would you?" Jilly muttered that babies don't attack you, but I could see that she was weakening. She's just a bit more cautious than I am. Some people would say, more sensible. Because it's true, if a dog is frightened it *can* bite you, just out of blind fear. I wouldn't have blamed poor darling Mud if he'd taken a snap at me, not one little bit. But being Mud, he didn't. He's not that sort of dog. He is just one big softie. Even after all he's been through.

With Jilly hanging onto the back of my jeans, in case I lost my balance and fell in, I squatted down on the edge of the ditch and reached out to the suitcase. I tugged at it, and heaved, and Jilly firmly hung onto me, but the thing had somehow gotten wedged and wouldn't move. All it did was sink a little farther into the mud.

The whimpers were beginning to grow really frantic, and so were Jilly and I.

"Unlock it, unlock it!" cried Jilly.

By now the suitcase was standing on one end, three-quarters submerged in the horrible black mud. One lock was out of the water and I was able to pry it open, but for the other I had to send my hand snaking deep down into the gunky depths. I have to tell you that I am the sort of person who feels sick just emptying my plate into the trash can in the school cafeteria. So putting my hand into that ditch was something I definitely did not enjoy. It was only the sound of that frantic whimpering that made me brave enough.

"Quick!" urged Jilly, as my fingers slipped and slimed through the squelchy ooze.

I found the second lock and slipped it back. Instantly, the suitcase burst open and Mud fell out, headfirst straight into the ditch. Next thing I knew, he was scrabbling out onto dry land, hauling himself up on great hairy legs like a spider's.

As soon as he was out, he shook himself.

brrrrrrrrrrrrr!

Huge lumps of mud flew everywhere. One went *splat!* Right into my eye. Jilly found this very amusing. (She'd had the sense to get out of the way.)

When he had finished shaking, Mud looked at us, bright eyed, as if ready for fun and games. Being locked in a suitcase and almost drowned didn't seem to have dampened his spirits one little bit. He is a really brave dog.

"What shall we do with him?" asked Jilly.

"Take him home," I said. My heart was already beginning to hammer and thud in my rib cage. I'd wanted a dog! I'd wanted a dog for ages. I'd asked Mom only the other day if we could have one and she'd promised that she would think about it.

"A Cocker Spaniel, perhaps. Or a Yorkshire Terrier. Something small and easy."

Mud wasn't a Cocker Spaniel, of course. And he certainly wasn't a Yorkshire Terrier. But he was a dog! And someone had tried to kill him, and he needed a home. How could Mom possibly say no? You would have to have a heart of *stone* to say no.

"We were going to get a dog," I said.

"Not one like that," said Jilly.

"Why not?" I put my hand on Mud, protectively. "What's wrong with him?"

I already felt that he belonged to me, and that I had to stick up for him.

"Well, I mean—," said Jilly.

"He's beautiful!"

"Yes, but he's . . ." Her voice trailed off.

"A dog is a dog," I said. "And I'm not just going to leave him!"

Even Jilly agreed that we couldn't just leave him. It's funny about Jilly, she never used to be a dog person before we found Mud. Not a real dog person. Like if we ever met one out on a walk, she'd never pet it or talk to it, unless maybe it was a puppy or something really tiny. It was because she was nervous. I wasn't! Not ever. I'd say hello to anything, even a Doberman or a German Shepherd, though of course you have to be careful. I guess I have always just instinctively known about dogs. Such as, for instance, how you should always hold out your hand, palm open, and touch them under the chin, not on top of the head. I don't know how I know this, but I do. And so does Jilly, now. Thanks to Mud!

When we first rescued him, she hadn't the faintest idea. She just stared at him, rather helplessly, and Mud stared back, through a fringe of gunked-up fur. I have to admit, he didn't look like the sort of dog to win any prizes. He was black from nose to tail, and he smelled. But it wasn't his fault.

"Poor doggy," I said, and he wagged his tail and splatted me a bit more.

"How do we get him to come?" asked Jilly. "Do you think he'll just follow?"

He might have done it, but we couldn't risk it. Cars came along the lane, and sometimes they came quite fast. We didn't want Mud getting run over! Not when we'd just rescued him.

Needless to say, he wasn't wearing any collar. Slimeballs who cram their dogs into suitcases and dump them in ditches don't usually bother about such things as collars.

"I wish I'd gotten the creep's number!" I said.

But it wasn't any good wishing. In the future, I swore an oath, I was going to train myself to be more observant. The next creep I saw trying to murder his dog wasn't going to get away with it.

For now, we had the problem of how to get Mud back with us. It was Jilly who had the bright idea that we should take off our socks and knot them together to make a collar, and that we should then take the laces out of our sneakers and knot *them* together to make a leash. So that was what we did.

Mud was so good! It was like he had already decided he was our dog. He let me put the sock collar around his neck and attach the shoelace leash, tied in a loop, and came trotting off with us as meek as could be. No problem!

We must have made a strange picture as we tramped back down the lane. There was me, leading a big hairy dog all covered in mud, shuffling in my undone sneakers, and there was Jilly, stomping ahead, trying her best to keep two bikes under control and not always succeeding.

It was a long walk home, and by the time we reached Riddlestone, I'd rubbed blisters on both my heels, but I didn't care. We'd saved Mud from a watery grave and there was just *no way* Mom could refuse to let me keep him.

Jilly said, "Don't count your chickens; I wouldn't," but she is always saying things like that. I didn't take any notice of her.

Chapter 2

As we trailed down High Street, Mud and me, and Jilly and the bikes, we could see that people were looking at us. Normally I'd have been quite embarrassed. I hate being looked at! Today it didn't bother me, because we'd rescued Mud. It gave me a warm glow inside. I kept looking at him trotting by my side, and thinking that if it hadn't been for me and Jilly he'd have been dead by now. So what did it matter if I was splattered all over in stinky black gunk and had blisters on both my heels? Who cared? Not me!

We cut across Parsley Green, which leads to Honeypot Lane, which is where we live. Honeypot Lane is a very short road without any pavement. There is just a row of cottages on one side and woods and fields on the other, and no garages, which means that Mom has to park the car outside. It drives her crazy because stuff from the trees falls on it—sticky stuff— and blotches up the windshield, but that is part of the price you pay for living in the country. Better than pollution, is what I say. And besides, I get paid to keep the windshield clear!

There are only four cottages in Honeypot Lane. Old Mr. Woodvine lives in the first one, and even older Mrs. Cherry in the second. Mr. Woodvine and Mrs. Cherry are real genuine country folk. Mrs. Cherry is about 90, I think. Both she and Mr. Woodvine were born and raised in Riddlestone. They think of us as "townies" and laugh when Mom carries on about her windshield.

Next to Mrs. Cherry is Jilly's mom, Mrs. Montague. She keeps a special cover over her car so the sticky stuff can't get on it. She is that sort of person. Mom (fortunately) is too busy and can't be bothered.

Jilly's mom was in her tiny little bit of front garden, kneeling on a special gardening mat and wearing her special gardening gloves. She's really particular, Jilly's mom. The minute she sees a weed poking itself above the ground, she's out there, yanking it up. Which I think is a pity, as some weeds are quite pleasant.

She glanced up and saw us as we turned onto the lane. Her mouth went into this big *O* and her eyes grew huge as dinner plates. It was quite comical, really. You'd have thought she'd spotted the blob-footed monster from Mars coming toward her.

"I hope you're not thinking of bringing that creature in here!" she cried.

Jilly said, "It's all right, Mom. We're taking him to Clara's."

We wouldn't have been stupid enough to try taking him into Jilly's. Jilly's mom is very fussy. She weeds her house like she weeds her garden. In our place it doesn't really matter too much if you spill things or break things, or drop crumbs on the carpet; Mom just tells you to wipe it up or get rid of it. Jilly's mom, on the other hand, goes berserk. I don't think she'll ever let Jilly have a dog: she isn't at all an animal person. Some people just aren't, which I think is sad.

Mrs. Montague got up off her gardening mat

and came over to the gate. She looked at Mud as if he were something that had crawled out of a garbage dump and said, "Is your mother actually expecting this, Clara?"

I said, "No, but she wants a dog."

"I see." Mrs. Montague pursed her lips. (She's always pursing her lips. It makes her look like she's just sucked a lemon.) "Well! Best of luck, that's all I can say."

She is a strange person. It's amazing that Jilly is so normal.

"It'll be all right," I said. "Mom won't mind." And I tugged on Mud's leash and clicked my tongue and said, "Come on, boy!" and Mud obediently stopped what he was doing (which was lifting his leg against Jilly's mom's fence, only she couldn't see it, thank goodness), and we went on up the lane, followed by Jilly and the bikes.

Jilly said, "Do you really think your mom won't mind?"

" 'Course she won't!" I said.

"It would be awful if we had to take him to the police."

"I'm not taking him to the police!" I was

horrified. How could she even suggest such a thing? Poor Mud! After all he'd been through! If he hadn't been quite so muddy, I'd have thrown my arms around his neck and hugged him. (Just to reassure him. I'm convinced dogs can understand more than people realize.)

"I'm not taking him anywhere," I said. "He's mine!"

"*Ours.*" Jilly sounded hurt.

"OK," I said. "Ours."

"We could share him," said Jilly. "He could live with you, but I could help take him for walks. If your mom says we can keep him."

Jilly is such a worrywart! She just didn't realize that my mom isn't like hers. Of course she'd let us keep him! I hadn't a doubt in my mind.

It just goes to show how even your own mom can let you down.

I wasn't terribly surprised when Mom opened the front door and shrieked, "What on earth have you got there?" because poor old Mud really did look a bit like a distant relative of the Loch Ness monster. All the same, I thought it was a bit foolish of Jilly to say, "It's a dog, Mrs. Carter."

Mom said, "I can see it's a dog! Where did you get it?"

I said, "We rescued him, Mom."

"Some creep—"

"Tried to drown him!"

"Threw him out of a car—"

"In a suitcase—"

"Into a ditch—"

"He'd have died, Mom, if we hadn't been there!"

There was a pause.

"You'd better bring him around the back," said Mom.

So we led Mud a bit farther on down the lane, up the side, and in through the back gate, and he came with us just as good as good can be, because he trusted us, me and Jilly. We'd rescued him from the ditch and he just knew we wouldn't do anything to hurt him.

Mom and Benjy were waiting for us in the back garden. Benjy is my little brother. He's eight and gets carsick a lot. When he saw Mud he said, "Ugh! Duddy!" which actually means dirty in Benjy-talk, not muddy as you might think.

I guess I ought to explain about Benjy. I mean, why he talks the way he does. It's because he has a problem hearing. He can lip-read really well, plus he has this hearing aid to help him; it's just that it isn't always easy for him to make the right sounds. He's supposed to practice with his lips pressed against a blown-up balloon. All the "explosives," as Mom calls them. "B-b-b-b-b-b" and "P-p-p-p-p-p," going off like popguns. He gets bored, though, and doesn't do it as much as he ought to, so that sometimes people have difficulty understanding him. I never do; I suppose because I'm used to it.

When he looked at Mud and said "Duddy," I told him that it wasn't Mud's fault.

"A nasty man threw him into a ditch."

"Wod he do dad for?"

"Because he was a *slimeball*," said Jilly.

Benjy loves that word. Slimeball. It always makes him chuckle. He said, "Dimebaw, dimebaw!" and Mud got excited and began jumping up and down. And as he jumped, he sprayed mud in all directions.

Benjy squealed and so did Jilly. She got splatted with mud all over her lovely clean *white* top! I suppose it was a bit mean of me, really, but I was sort of pleased about that. I mean, I'd been in a mud bath, why shouldn't she? After all, she was the one who'd said we'd share.

"Ugh! Yuck!" said Jilly, wiping mud out of her eye.

"You can say that again," agreed Mom. "Let's get him cleaned up."

What a job it was! We filled the watering can, a bucket, and the dishpan with warm water, and Benjy fetched his special baby shampoo from the bathroom (Benjy has to use baby shampoo because he has this very sensitive skin, which Mom said dogs have, too). Jilly put on Mom's plastic apron and held Mud, while Mom poured the water, and I soaped and squeezed, and the mud ran away in rivulets.

The minute we'd finished, Mud shook himself—*brrrrrrrrr!*—just as he had when he'd clambered out of the ditch. This time, everybody got wet. But at least it was clean water.

After that, Jilly and I dried him off with a couple of bath towels, and we all stood back to admire him. He was really quite handsome! Well, I thought so. I didn't care what anybody said.

Benjy wanted to know if he was a "Dob Byler." He meant Rottweiler.

Mom said, "No, he looks to me like your complete mongrel."

"*Pedigree* mongrel," said Jilly.

(As she explained to me afterward, when I was trying to explain that you couldn't have a pedigree mongrel, "I know, but I didn't want him to feel hurt." That was when I knew she was turning into a real dog person!)

"I suppose," Mom said doubtfully, "he might have a bit of wolfhound in him."

He had the long hairy legs of a wolfhound and his coat was right: a sort of sandy color (when it wasn't covered in mud) and quite wiry.

"He's terribly thin," said Mom. "Poor boy!" She held out a hand and Mud snuffled eagerly. "I wonder if he's hungry?"

25

"Let's give him some food!"

Of course, we didn't have any proper dog food, but Mud didn't seem to mind. We took him into the kitchen and he ate his way through one can of beef stew, half a pack of cookies, two slices of whole wheat bread, a licorice candy (generously donated by Benjy), and a big bowl of milk. We watched in awe as he gobbled it all down.

"He must have been absolutely starving," said Jilly. "I bet the creep didn't feed him!"

That was when Mom asked us if we'd gotten the license plate number of the car and we had to admit that we hadn't, and didn't even know what make it was.

"Never mind," said Mom. "You did a splendid job in rescuing him. I'm proud of you! Both of you."

Jilly and I preened. Benjy said, "I'd've wedcued him, too!"

"Yes, I'm sure you would," said Mom, soothingly. "You'd have been just as brave as Jilly and Clara. Now! We have to decide what we're going to do with him."

When Mom said that, Jilly looked at me and

26

I looked at Jilly, and Jilly mouthed, "*Ask her!*" And I said, "Couldn't we keep him, Mom? You said you wanted a dog."

Mom laughed. She actually laughed! She said, "Not a dog like this. Look at the size of him!"

We both turned to look at Mud. He was standing with his lovely whiskery head on the kitchen table, trying to check out if there was any more grub.

"He doesn't look that big to me," I said.

"He's the size of a small horse!" said Mom. "And for all we know, he hasn't even finished growing."

That was when Jilly made her mistake. She said, "He couldn't still be a puppy, could he? Not that size?" Thus betraying the fact that she was very well aware Mud was, well, somewhat larger than a Cocker Spaniel.

"But he isn't *big*," I said quickly, with a warning frown at Jilly. "It's only that his legs are long." The hideous slimeball that had tried to drown him must have bent them up when he crammed Mud into the suitcase. "He's what I'd call *tall*," I said, "rather than big."

"Yes, and likely to grow even taller," said Mom.

I felt my lip begin to quiver. I hadn't expected this of Mom!

"We rescued him," I said.

"Clara, I know you did! I've already told you, I'm very proud of you. But you must see, we couldn't possibly keep a dog that size. Apart from anything else, he'd eat us out of house and home."

"I'd help feed him," said Jilly. "I'd buy him dog food out of my pocket money."

"We'd share him, Mom! We'd both look after him."

"You mean, he'd live part of the time here and part of the time at Jilly's?" said Mom.

Jilly gnawed at her bottom lip. I looked at Mom, reproachfully. She knew perfectly well that Jilly's mom would never have a dog in the house.

"I'd take him for walks," said Jilly.

"We'd both take him for walks. Twice a day, Mom!"

Mom shook her head. "I'm sorry, girls. There's just no way. I can't possibly have an animal that size in a place as small as this."

Mom has a thing about the house being small. It's true that where we live now would fit into just about one room, probably, of where we used to live before, but on the other hand, where we lived before hardly had any garden at all, whereas now we have acres. Well, say, a couple of acres. Say, *half* an acre. But that is still quite big. Plenty big enough for a dog like Mud.

I said this to Mom, but she said, "Clara, I don't think you realize how much exercise a dog of this size would need."

"But I told you! We'd take him for walks!"

"And what happens during the day, when you and Jilly are at school?"

"I'd take him for a walk *before* school and then he could go in the garden."

"Look," said Mom. "It may be all very well in this weather, when we can leave the back door open and he could run in and out all day, but what happens in winter? When it's cold and wet—and muddy? What does he do then?"

"He'd sleep by the fireplace!" I said.

"Yes, and every time he got up or turned around—"

Mom suddenly broke off.

"What are you doing?" she cried.

Mud had jumped onto the table! We all sprang at it together. Another second, and the whole thing would have tipped over, with disastrous results.

"You naughty boy!" scolded Mom. "Get down this instant!"

She didn't really sound mad, but it spelled the end of Mud's chances.

"You see what I mean?" said Mom. "He is just *too big*."

There was a long silence, then Jilly, in a small voice, said, "So what's going to happen to him?" I couldn't trust myself to speak. I knew if I did I'd burst into tears, and I'd have been ashamed to do that in front of Jilly and Benjy.

"Well . . ." Mom said it carefully. "We could either take him to the police station—"

"*No!*" That was Jilly and me together. Even if I did burst into tears I knew I couldn't let Mom take Mud to the police.

"Please," begged Jilly. "Please, Mrs. Carter!"

I think we both had visions of poor darling Mud being shut up in a cell, or more likely a horrid cold kennel in a concrete yard.

"All right," said Mom. "The other thing we could do is take him to an animal shelter."

"What would happen to him there?" asked Jilly. I noticed that her voice didn't sound too steady.

"They'd find a home for him," said Mom. "A better home than this."

I choked. "There couldn't be a better home than this!"

"A bigger home," said Mom. "One where he could move around in comfort."

"But he *is* comfortable!" I said.

Mud had stretched out on the kitchen floor, the picture of doggy bliss. I have to admit he took up half the kitchen, but so what? It was easy enough to step over him.

"Let me call the police," said Mom, "and see if they can give me a number."

The police told Mom there was an animal shelter called End of the Line right nearby, in

Riddlestone itself.

"Practically on the doorstep," said Mom.

Jilly and I didn't say anything.

"I'll go and give them a call," Mom announced. "It would be best, really, if we could get him down there right away, before you get too attached to him."

We were already attached to him! I couldn't bear the thought of Mud being carted off to an animal shelter. He was so happy with us! Benjy was down on the floor, smooching over him, and Mud was on his back, his legs gangling, his tongue lolling out, loving every minute of it. *He* didn't know that Mom was on the phone, arranging to get rid of him.

The tears rolled miserably down my cheeks and went plopping off my chin. How could Mom do such a thing?

"Dide og," said Benjy.

Mud's tail thumped in agreement.

"Did he say *guide* dog?" asked Jilly.

"Nice dog." I blew my nose. Jilly looked at me sympathetically. This was even worse for me than it was for her, because it was my mom who was doing it. Jilly was really good; she never once said "I told you so." I would have done it, if I'd been her.

Mom came back and said, "OK! They can take him tomorrow morning. I said we'd hang on to him until then."

"Oh! Mom! *Thank* you!"

I hurled myself at her, but she fended me off.

"I don't want you getting up any false hopes, Clara. I meant what I said. He's far too big for us to keep."

But at least he could stay until the morning. It was impossible not to feel just a *tiny* ray of hope.

Chapter 3

Oh, dear! Mud did everything he could to destroy that little ray of hope. Not that he could know; he was just being Mud. Just enjoying himself. Being happy.

To begin with, right after Mom had finished calling the police and the animal shelter, he went and disgraced himself by upsetting her coffee, which she made specially with warm milk (yuck!) the way she likes it. Mom really goes overboard about her coffee. Mom's coffee is, like, *sacred*. And Mud had to go jumping up at just the wrong moment and send it flying!

She got really mad. She yelled, "Clara, get that dog out of here!"

I yanked at Mud and ran into the garden. Mud seemed to think it was some kind of game; he wasn't the least bit bothered by Mom yelling at him. When she came out a few minutes later to make up (Mom always makes up when she's lost her temper), I thought perhaps he'd shrink away from her. I imagined in his doggy mind he'd be thinking, "That's the woman who shouted at me. I'd better keep away from her."

But no! He saw Mom—with another cup of coffee in her hand—and went bounding toward her. Mom just managed to whisk the cup out of the way in time, or that would have been a second one gone. I dread to think what would have happened *then*.

"What a big clumsy mutt you are!" said Mom. "I told you, you see . . . he's far too big for a house like this."

My heart sank. Jilly, trying to be helpful and just going and putting her foot in it again like she did earlier, said solemnly, "But he's in the garden now, Mrs. Carter, and the garden is *huge*."

"Yes!" said Mom. "So if he's still a big clumsy mutt in the garden, imagine how much worse he'll be indoors!"

I gave Jilly this fierce glare, which shut her up.

"He's just excited," I said to Mom, "because of everything being all new and different."

Mom said, "Well! In that case I suggest you keep him out here for a bit and run some of the wind out of his tail."

He shouldn't really have had any wind left in his tail when you consider that he'd walked all the way back from Feather Down Lane with us, but that little sprawl on the kitchen floor seemed to have replenished his energy.

We spent the next hour before lunch exploring the garden, where fortunately he couldn't do too much damage because of the garden being mostly just trees and bushes. Mom keeps saying she's going to "get around to it," though personally I like it the way it is. I find flowers a bit annoying because you are forever being told not to trample on them or crush them or throw your ball into them. Grown-ups get neurotic about flowers in a way they don't about trees and bushes.

The only bad thing Mud did in the garden was to snatch a bit of Mom's washing off the line and go tearing off across the grass with it, with me and Jilly in hot pursuit. Unfortunately, that rotten little snitch Benjy had to go running indoors to tell her. We heard him bellowing, "Mom, Mom!" (Mom is one of the words he always says properly.) "Dob dodda woddin!"

Actually, to be fair to Benjy, he didn't mean to snitch. He just thought it was funny. He wanted Mom to come and enjoy the joke.

Mom thought it was quite funny at first—until she saw what it was that Mud had snatched. A pair of her panty hose! A *good* pair. (Now that we don't have much money, Mom has good pairs and bad pairs. Good pairs are ones without any holes, or holes in places where you can't see them. Bad pairs are the sort she only wears indoors, or under jeans.)

When she saw that it was *good* panty hose trailing out of the side of Mud's mouth, she flew into a sort of hysteria and yelled, "Stop him, stop him! Bad dog! Stay!"

It was like she'd never spoken. Mud just went right on galloping. Around and around the garden he galloped, ears flapping and tail streaming, and Mom's panty hose clamped between his jaws.

Jilly and I did our best. We chased him all

around, alternately pleading with him— "*Good* boy! *Good* boy!" and yelling at him—"*Bad* boy! *Stay!*"

Mud took absolutely no notice whatsoever.

In the end, the panty hose caught on a bush as Mud went careening past, and that was that: farewell to Mom's good panty hose!

It is just as well that Mom is not a violent person. Well, I mean, if she were I'd have been clobbered more times than I could count. But she doesn't believe in hitting children or animals. All she said, rather wearily, as Jilly and I managed to remove what was left of the panty hose from Mud's mouth, was, "I told you he'd eat us out of house and home."

"We'll buy you another pair," said Jilly, earnestly.

I said, "He was only playing, Mom! He thought it was a game."

"Some game!" said Mom. And then, rather irritably to Mud, "What's the matter with you, you stupid mutt? Are you crazy, or something?"

Mud wagged, amiably. I said, "Mom! He couldn't have known."

"Couldn't have known what *stay* means?"

"He's probably never been taught," I said.

"He shouldn't have to be taught! He should be able to pick it up from the tone of your voice. And he can stop waving that ridiculous tail at me! I'm afraid I don't think much of his intelligence," said Mom. "He's obviously not very bright."

"Dod bery bride," crooned Benjy, throwing his arms round Mud's neck. "Baw doddie! Dod bery bride."

I thought that was a really mean thing for Mom to say. She wasn't even giving Mud a chance!

Jilly went back home to have her lunch, and we agreed that afterward we would take Mud for a walk in the hope of making him so tired he would lie down and go to sleep.

"That way," I said, "he'll seem like a *good* dog. A good *quiet* dog. It's his only hope."

He disgraced himself again at lunchtime by coming right up and swiping a potato off Benjy's plate.

"I don't believe this!" said Mom. "Clara, shut him in the garden with a handful of plain cookies."

So Mud spent lunchtime in the garden, and while he was out there took the opportunity to dig a few really good holes in places where people were likely to stumble over them in the dark and break their ankles. Jilly and I had to spend ages filling them in again before Mom would let us go off for our walk.

"Maybe he's a digging dog," said Jilly. "Like for digging foxes out."

"Don't!" I said. "That's horrid!" Even then I hated people who hunt foxes.

We still didn't have a proper leash for Mud, but Mom said that we could use one of her old belts.

"And I'd keep him on it, if I were you, if you don't want to run the risk of losing him."

We took Mud across the lane and into the woods. Jilly said to me, "That's a good sign, what she just said . . . don't you think?"

I sighed; I wasn't so sure. Jilly hadn't heard about the potato incident.

"I mean, about not losing him," urged Jilly. "I mean, if she's not going to keep him, why should she care if we lose him?"

"Because she doesn't want anything bad to

happen to him," I said.

"Even if she's not going to keep him?"

"It's like she gives money to the RSPCA. For the animals. They're not *her* animals, but she still wants them to be happy." The RSPCA is the Royal Society for the Prevention of Cruelty to Animals, just like the ASPCA back in America.

"Oh."

We walked for a while in silence, then Jilly said, "So you don't think she's going to change her mind?"

"*I* don't know!" I swished angrily at a passing tree. What made me angry was that I had a horrid feeling I might be going to start crying again. I didn't want to do that; not in front of Jilly. I hate crying in front of people.

"Let's let him off," I said, "and see if he'll walk to heel."

"Oh, but, Clara, do you think we ought to?" quavered Jilly. "He might run away!"

Mud didn't show any signs of wanting to run away. He seemed to regard himself as our dog. I didn't think there was any harm in just letting him off the leash.

41

"But your mom—," began Jilly.

"Mom doesn't know everything! Don't be such a baby," I said, and I undid the belt and slapped a hand against my thigh. "Heel!" I said. "Good boy! Heel!"

We walked in a big circle, right through the woods and around the edge of the field on the far side. Every now and again Mud would make little darts into the undergrowth in search of wild life. The first few times he did it even I got worried and went running after him, but he always came back, and so in the end we got used to it. I suppose we stopped watching him quite so closely because suddenly Jilly said, "Where is he?" and we found to our horror that he had gone.

"He was here a second ago," I said. "He can't have gone far."

We went racing off into the woods, yelling at him to come back. We hadn't actually given him the name Mud at that stage, so all we could shout was "Good boy!" or "Good dog!"

Jilly kept crying that he was lost and that we'd never find him again.

"We shouldn't have let him off! Your mom

was right, I knew she was!"

It really got on my nerves, because I knew she was, too. If Mud were lost, it would be all my fault. So I told Jilly rather fiercely to shut up. I said that whining didn't help. I said, "Let's just *stop* for a moment and *listen*."

We stood there, straining our ears, but all we could hear were birds chattering in the trees. And then I caught sight of something sandy colored come flashing out from a clump of holly bushes and go galloping off down a far distant path. I yelled, "There he is!" and we set off after him, desperately calling as we went.

"Good boy, good boy! Over here! Good boy!"

Mud didn't take the slightest bit of notice; he just went on galloping. Jilly was in tears and I was terrified because he was heading for the main road. Oh, why didn't he *stop*?

We didn't have a chance of catching him: He was too far ahead and he was moving too fast. It was only in desperation that I snatched up a knobbly chunk of wood from the ground and hurled it at him. I am not actually a very good shot (I have *no* ball sense; Miss Hyatt at school says I am totally useless) so no one was more surprised than I when the chunk of wood caught Mud on the shoulder and went bouncing off him. Well, maybe Mud was, because he stopped dead in his tracks and spun around to see who was chucking things at him. And when he saw that it was Jilly and me, he gave this great big happy grin and came bouncing right back to us. And Jilly and I were so relieved that we threw our arms around him before we realized that he was covered all over in mud . . . *again*! He must have found a really muddy patch and wallowed in it.

"Oh! That's the second top I've ruined!" wailed Jilly. "My mom's going to be so mad!"

"It doesn't matter," I said. "We've got him back, that's all that matters."

But I wasn't taking any more chances: I put him on his leash for the rest of the walk.

"Though I don't think he was actually running away from us," I said. "I think he was trying to find us."

"So why didn't he come when we called?"

"Well, because we don't know what his name is," I said. "If we'd known what his name was, he'd probably have come."

Mom and Benjy were both in the garden when we arrived home. Mom was sitting in a chair in the sunshine reading her Sunday paper. Benjy was doing little boy things with his toy cars, vrr-vrrming them and racing them up and down a plank of wood. When he saw Mud he broke into delighted peals of laughter and cried, "Dub! Dub!"

"What?" said Mom. She peered out from behind her page. "Oh, for heaven's sake! Not again?"

"Dub!" said Benjy. "He'd a dub dod!"

"Yes," I said. "It's obviously his breed. That's what he is: a mud dog."

And that was when we started calling him Mud.

After we'd cleaned him up for the second time, Mud was pretty tired and decided to retire to the cabinet under the sink. First of all he threw out all the stuff that was already in there. All the pots, pans, cans of furniture polish and turtle wax for the car, they were all sent scattering across the kitchen floor while Mud made a nest for himself in a pile of old cleaning rags and went to sleep. Mom said, "At least he's quiet."

He stayed quiet for about an hour, until it was dinner time, when he came out with his nose twitching and swiped a can of tuna fish that Mom had foolishly left open on the edge of the kitchen countertop. I just managed to scrape the tuna off the floor and stuff it back in the can before she appeared, but I didn't have time to wipe up the oily mess, and Mom went and stepped in it before I could warn her.

"*Clara*," she said, "if that is that dog—"

"No," I said, "it was me! I was going to put the tuna on a plate for you only I went and dropped it."

I don't know whether Mom believed me or not.

Jilly had to go home for her own dinner, which meant she wouldn't see Mud again until morning.

"And then it will only be to say good-bye," she said mournfully.

"Oh, now, come on, Jilly!" said Mom. "I never heard of you wanting a dog."

"I didn't before we found Mud," said Jilly,

and she turned her big blue eyes on Mom and gave her the sort of look that would have melted stone.

It didn't melt Mom. She said, "Wait till we have our Cocker Spaniel! You'll love him just as much. And Mud will be perfectly well looked after at the shelter."

Mom must have a heart of *granite*.

Later that evening Jilly called to say that she was about to go to bed but knew she wouldn't be able to settle down until she had checked how Mud was. I said that he was OK, he was asleep on the rug.

"Like a real dog."

"He is a real dog!" said Jilly.

"I mean a normal dog." A dog that didn't steal panty hose and swipe cans of tuna and jump onto tables and help himself to potatoes and dig holes in the garden and get covered in mud twice in one day. Not that the first time had been Mud's fault.

Jilly said, "Don't normal dogs do the sort of things that Mud does?"

"Well . . . perhaps not all at one time. I mean, like, they might stretch them out a bit.

Dig up the garden one day and steal panty hose the next day. Not all on the *same* day."

"I see," said Jilly. And then, in pleading tones, "But he hasn't done anything else? Not since dinner time?"

I said not really—just wagged his tail a bit too energetically and swept a glass off Benjy's supper tray.

"Oh! Well, that's not too bad," said Jilly.

"It was full of milk," I said.

"Oh," said Jilly. She sighed. "Poor Mud!"

When it came to bedtime (I am allowed to go to bed an hour later than Jilly), I asked Mom if Mud could come and sleep with me, but she said no (heart of *granite*), he was going to be shut away in the kitchen. She said he would be quite happy.

"He can always go back in his cabinet. He seems to like it in there."

Mud might have liked his cabinet during the day, but he didn't like it at night. It was about 11:00 when I heard Mom come upstairs to bed, and about ten minutes later when Mud started to whimper. I went into Mom's bedroom and said, "Mom! He's crying."

"He'll stop," said Mom.

I gave it five minutes and then went back again.

"He's still doing it, Mom!"

Mom said, "Clara I am not having you bring him upstairs."

"But he's lonely!" I said. "He needs company!"

"He'll survive," said Mom.

Grown-ups can be so mean at times. Mom would never have let Benjy lie in bed and cry. She never did. She always used to go running. But with poor Mud, she just didn't care.

"He's a *dog*," she said.

But dogs can get lonely and frightened, just the same as people.

At midnight Mud started howling and I just couldn't stand it. I pulled on my bathrobe and picked up a pillow and the comforter, and went creeping out onto the landing. Mom had switched her light off and I thought she was probably asleep, but I skimmed down the stairs on tiptoe, holding my breath at every creak.

Mud was so happy to see me! He hurled himself at me in a frenzy, yipping with joy. I said, "Shsh!" and put a finger to my lips. I didn't want Mom waking up and wondering what all the noise was about.

I put my pillow on the floor, wrapped myself up in the comforter and lay down. Mud instantly lay down with me. We spent the rest of the night snuggled together.

Chapter 4

We were still curled up together, me and Mud, when Mom came down next morning to make a cup of coffee. Mud had one of his legs stretched across my neck, and his nose tucked under my chin, and was so sound asleep (making little whiffling noises) that he didn't wake up even when Mom said, "Clara! How long have you been down here?"

I said, "Since midnight," hoping that she would feel really guilty about it.

"Oh, you are a silly girl!" said Mom.

"I had to," I said. "I couldn't just let him go on crying. He was so unhappy down here all by himself!"

At that moment Mud woke up and saw Mom. He immediately flipped over onto his back and began whirring his paws around his head. Even Mom had to laugh.

"He was really miserable," I said.

"He's manipulative," said Mom. "Knows how to get his own way. Don't you?" And she crouched down and tickled Mud's tummy, which sent him into ecstasy. "Slopbag!" said Mom.

For a wonderful, blissful moment I honestly thought that Mom was going to give in and say that she had changed her mind, and that we could keep him after all. How could anyone resist a dog as sweet as Mud? He was trying so hard! He was telling Mom as plain as could be that he wanted to stay with us.

"He's a dog who'll always land on his feet," said Mom. "You don't have to worry about him."

"But he's already had an owner who tried to drown him!" I said. "Suppose they send him back to the same man?"

"They wouldn't do that," said Mom.

"How would they know? If he just came in and said he wanted a dog, and he chose Mud . . . they wouldn't know he was the one who tried to drown him!"

"Stop torturing yourself," said Mom. "It's not going to happen."

"How do you know it's not going to happen? You're just saying that! You don't know! You could be sending Mud to his *death*!"

"Clara." Mom said it gently, but at the same time in her listen-to-me-and-just-try-to-be-sensible voice. "The people at the shelter are highly experienced, they deal with dozens of dogs every week. They always check most carefully before they let anybody adopt one. Nothing bad is going to happen to Mud! Now, off you go and get dressed or you'll be late for school."

It was all Mom cared about. Me being late for school. She didn't care about poor Mud being handed over to strangers. Being sent to a doggy orphanage to live in a cage!

I stomped ill-temperedly up the stairs, hating Mom and full of forebodings about what the future might hold for Mud. Benjy was coming out of his room, fiddling with his hearing aid. (He hated wearing his hearing aid at first but he's quite good about it now because he realizes that it helps him.) He said, "Where'd Dub?"

"Downstairs," I said. "I've been sleeping with him all night because he was so unhappy. And now he's going to be made even more unhappy!"

Of course Benjy wanted to know why.

"Because Mom's getting rid of him!" I said. "She doesn't want him, so she's throwing him out. She's taking him to an orphanage where he'll have to live in a *cage*."

Benjy's face crumpled.

"He's going to feel we've abandoned him," I said. "He'll think we don't love him!"

"I lub him!" said Benjy.

"Yes, and so do I," I said. "But Mud couldn't know that."

I shouldn't have poured it all out onto Benjy. He was too young, really, to understand. But I was just so miserable, I had to dump some of it.

When I went back downstairs Benjy was sitting on the floor with Mud, his arms around his neck and his head buried in his fur. He was whispering to him.

"Baw, Dub, baw, Dub! Bendy lub you, Dub!"

Mom was at the stove, doing her best to pretend it wasn't happening. (Heart of *granite*.) She said, "Are you ready for your breakfast, Clara?" And then, suddenly banging a plate onto the table, she said, "I will not be black-mailed! Why did you have to go and upset your brother?"

I muttered, "Well, *I'm* upset."

"So you have to go and upset everyone else? You're being very unfair! Very selfish. Just try thinking of it from someone else's point of view. I'm the one who has to keep this house clean. When do you ever lift a finger? Never, unless I nag at you! I'm the one who has to earn enough money to feed us all and keep you in sneakers and stereos and—"

"I don't want a stereo!" I said. It's true I *had* wanted one, but that was before Mud had come into my life. I didn't care about stereos any-more. Or sneakers. I'd go around in bare feet if it meant I could keep Mud.

But Mom wasn't to be moved. It seemed the more I pleaded, the more determined she became. I could see in the end that I wasn't going to get anywhere. I was just making her more angry. I hate Mom being angry, even though I know it's quite often me that provokes her.

I suppose in some ways I am quite a provoking sort of person. But I can't help it! I don't mean to be. There's just something about me that gets people prickly.

We ate breakfast in stony silence—well, Mom and I ate in stony silence. Benjy kept up a stream of conversation directed at Mud— "Bendy lub you! Bendy lub you a *lot*" —while Mud sat with his head on Benjy's knee being fed mini-wheats and pieces of toast. Mom just concentrated on eating her breakfast and didn't say a word.

Usually Jilly and I meet at our front gates when it's time to go to school, but today she knocked at the door because she wanted to say good-bye to Mud. I went to let her in and hissed, "Don't say anything to Mom! She's in a mood."

Jilly's eyes widened, apprehensively. She whispered, "Why? What's happened?"

"It's because of Mud."

"Oh, no! Don't tell me he's done something else!"

"*He* hasn't done anything. It's Mom, sending him away. She's feeling guilty and it's making her mean."

I took Jilly through to the kitchen where Mud was busily licking the cereal bowls. Jilly, nervously, said, "Good morning, Mrs. Carter."

All tight-lipped (I bet she thought Jilly was going to start in on her, as well) Mom said, "Good morning, Jilly."

"I've just come to . . . um . . . say good-bye to Mud," said Jilly.

Mom waved a hand. "He's all yours."

I said, "I wish he was!" and burst into tears before I could stop myself. So then Jilly also burst into tears and we both stood there, weeping like water spouts, while Mud licked his cereal bowls, and Benjy in mournful tones chanted, "*Baw*, Dub, *baw*, Dub."

"Oh, for goodness' sake!" cried Mom. "What is this? A wailing wall? Just stop it, all of you!"

The thing about Mom is, she can never stay in a mood for very long. As she came to the door to see us off (after we'd both kissed Mud and promised that we would never, ever forget him) she said, "Look, I'm sorry, girls, I know you're upset, and it does seem hard when you were so brave in rescuing him, but you must see that he really is *far* too big. I know he'll find a good home for himself! People will take one look and they won't be able to resist him. I bet you anything you like he'll be adopted before the week is out!"

She was doing her best to make us feel better, but Mud never left our thoughts all day long. We kept imagining Mom driving up to the shelter and Mud thinking she was taking him for a walk and then discovering the awful truth: She was leaving him there! We wondered if he would feel hurt. If he would miss us. If he would wait patiently for Mom to come and take him back again, without realizing that she wasn't ever going to.

Every now and again we would imagine such terrible, heartrending scenes that we would both start sniffling and blowing our noses, and everyone would politely look the other way because it is *so* shameful to be caught crying in public. Except just this one girl, Geraldine Hooper, who is our sworn enemy and has a face like an old squashed mushroom. She came up and, all gloating, she said, "What's the matter with you two? Won't little old Eriky Weriky talk to you anymore?"

She suffers from this dreadful raging jealousy, all because Erik the Gorgeous once spoke real words to us. It was when we were hanging around one day waiting to get a glimpse of him, and he appeared unexpectedly through a door and almost squashed us flat. He said, "Hey, sorry! You OK?" and he *touched* us. Well, he touched Jilly. He put a hand on her shoulder, and Geraldine Hopper was there and she saw it, so she couldn't say we were making it up. She's been green with jealousy ever since, but anyway, her loathsome, repulsive sarcasm was totally wasted since all our thoughts were with Mud. Gorgeous Erik really didn't mean a thing to us anymore. (I suppose you could say we were a bit fickle but Mud *needed* us.)

Jilly really rose to the occasion. She put on this incredible grand lady voice and said, "What on earth are you burbling about, you silly little girl?" *That* put Geraldine Hooper in her place.

"I wasn't going to tell her about Mud," Jilly said to me later, as we wandered arm in arm around the playground at recess.

"No," I said. "I couldn't bear to tell anyone about Mud."

When we got home that afternoon, Mom was waiting for us, all beams and smiles and trying to bribe us with a special meal she'd prepared. She said, "Come on, Jilly! You're invited. I've checked with your mom."

While we were eating (which was absolutely delicious—she must have been feeling *really* guilty) Mom told us about the shelter. She said that it was perfect, and the woman who ran it was perfect, and all the girls who worked there were perfect. *Everything* was perfect, and Mud was going to be fine.

"They don't think they'll have any trouble finding him a new home, he's got such a great temperament. And they reckon he's only about nine months old, which means, you see, that he *could* still grow bigger. But it's good that he's so young because young dogs are what people mostly want. Oh, and they said that if you liked, you could go and visit him after school

and take him for a walk. They're always looking for people to help exercise the dogs. I said
I'd ask you. What do you think? Would it upset
you too much or would you like to do that?
You could easily bicycle there from school.
Then you could see for yourselves what a great
place it is. It might set your minds at rest."

At first I thought I couldn't bear it, going to
visit Mud and then having to leave him again.
It would be like visiting someone in prison.
But then Jilly pointed out that I was just thinking of me, and not of Mud. She said that if we
didn't go and take him for a walk he might not
get enough exercise, because he was a big dog
and he needed exercise, and the more he had,
the more he would be able to settle down in
between times and sleep while he waited for
someone to adopt him.

I knew she was right, so I said to Mom that
we would go the next day after school, and
Mom promised to call up the shelter and tell
them. She said, "The woman who runs the
place is named Meg Sanderson. You'll like her,
she's really nice. She really cares about the animals. I'm sure you'll feel a lot better when

you've been there."

In one way, I suppose, she was right. In one way we did feel better because of seeing for ourselves that everyone at the shelter was a real animal person and loved all the poor abandoned mutts and cats that were there. But in another way, Mom was quite wrong. In another way, we felt even worse than we had before.

To begin with it was all right, because Meg (she said to call her Meg, even though she was at least Mom's age) met us at the gate and was really friendly. She told us what a beautiful dog Mud was and how lucky he was that we had rescued him, what a splendid job we'd done, and how she wished there were more kids like us around. She took us into the yard, where there was this big enclosure with about 20 dogs inside, all shapes and sizes, and all waiting for people to adopt them. Some of the dogs were sleeping and some were running around, and it didn't look too bad because at least they weren't shut up in tiny little cages, which was what I'd feared. But Mud wasn't among them!

"Where is he?" asked Jilly.

"Mud's over here," said Meg, "with the newcomers."

And she took us across the yard to where there was a line of kennels, and there was poor Mud, shut away all by himself behind some chicken wire. He was just standing there, drooping, with his tail tucked between his legs, the picture of misery. When we'd said good-bye to him the day before he'd been so happy and bouncy! I just couldn't believe it.

Meg said soothingly, "It takes them a while to get used to it. He's still adapting."

"Why does he have to be by himself?" cried Jilly, "Why can't he go in with the others?"

"He will, in time, if he's here long enough. Hopefully, he won't be. But we have to keep him isolated just at first. For one thing, we don't know if he's had his shots."

Jilly didn't know what shots were, and even I wasn't quite sure, so Meg explained about diseases like distemper and the parvovirus. She said that all the dogs had to be injected against them because they could spread like wildfire and were highly dangerous. But Mud had now had his shots, and as soon as they'd started to work he could go and be sociable.

"In the meantime, if you'd like to give him a bit of a run, I'm sure he'd love it."

It wasn't until Meg unlocked the door of his kennel that Mud looked up and realized we were there. The minute he saw us he went mad, bucking and prancing and making little squealing noises of doggy delight.

"He remembers us!" said Jilly. It was Jilly who was doing most of the talking. I had this huge lump in my throat that made it impossible.

"Of course he does!" said Meg. "He knows you were the people who rescued him." She clipped on his leash and held it out. "Just take him down the lane and into the field and then you can let him off. He'll be quite safe in there. Here!" She pulled a ball from her pocket. "Throw this for him. That will tire him out."

We gave Mud as good a time as we possibly could, throwing his ball and chasing and playing, but we couldn't do it nearly as long as he'd have liked because we'd promised our moms faithfully that we would be home by 5:00. It was really hard, having to take him back. Even harder having to leave him.

Meg gave him a handful of dog biscuits and said that he would settle down now that he'd had his run. We kissed him and whispered that we would see him again tomorrow, but of course there is no way for a dog to understand. All Mud knew was that we were abandoning him again.

Jilly turned to take one last look as we left the yard (I was too much of a coward). She reported that Mud was standing in his kennel, pressed against the chicken wire, "Gazing after us."

"He trusted us," I said, "and we've betrayed him!"

"It wasn't our fault," said Jilly.

"He couldn't know that!"

"No, I know," said Jilly, and she took out her handkerchief, which was already crumpled into a wet ball, and wiped her eyes. "But we're doing what we can!"

I suppose it should have been a comfort, but it wasn't much of one. I lay awake half the night thinking of Mud alone in his kennel. Sometimes life is really unfair, especially to dumb animals.

Chapter 5

We went to the shelter again the next day, and again the day after that. It was a little bit easier now that we knew what to expect, but not very much. Poor Mud was still in his cage, still drooping. He really did want to go and be with the others! And he wanted a proper home, where people would play with him and cuddle him.

"Like we would have done," said Jilly.

I sighed. "It isn't any use. Mom isn't ever going to let us have him."

Jilly could hardly say how mean and rotten Mom was, considering her mom wouldn't even let Mud go into the house, but I knew that she felt let down. Mom had turned out to be a disappointment! We had both thought better of her.

Each time we visited, Mud greeted us like

long-lost friends, jumping and squeaking and turning in circles.

"He is the most lovable animal," said Meg. "I'm sure it won't be long before somebody takes him."

"You won't let him go to just anyone," I pleaded, "will you?"

"Good gracious, no! We don't let any of our dogs go to just anyone."

Meg assured us that Mud wouldn't be going anywhere until she had done a home visit and checked what sort of house he would be living in and whether there was a yard he would be safe in and that all the family, even including tiny children, were going to get along with him.

"Nobody could get along with him like we do," I said.

"No, because you have a special relationship with him," agreed Meg. "When you've rescued a dog, you feel extra protective toward it. It's sad you can't keep him, but fortunately Mud is the sort of dog who is very easy to love. And we know he's good with children, because your mom told us how well he got along with your little brother."

"Yes, he did," I said. I remembered Benjy throwing his arms round Mud's neck and crooning, "Bendy lub you, Dub!" I still couldn't believe that Mom could be so cold-hearted.

"You mustn't blame your mom," said Meg. "I'll let you in on a secret, if you promise on your honor not to tell her . . . do you promise?"

Jilly and I nodded solemnly.

"Your mom," said Meg, "was in tears when she left Mud here. She found it just as difficult as you do to say good-bye to him. You probably think she was being harsh, but she was only doing what she thought was best for Mud. One of the worst things that can happen to a dog is to be taken in by a family and a few weeks later they decide they can't keep him and he ends up back in the kennels. Can you imagine what it's like for a dog when that happens? Just as he thinks he's found a home for himself, he's suddenly booted out all over again. Your mom didn't want that happening to Mud."

"But it had already happened!" I said. "He'd already been with us for a whole day!"

"Not long enough for him to decide that you

68

were his new people. Don't worry! Someone will adopt him very soon. I just wish I could say the same about some of the others."

Meg told us that there were some poor dogs who had been so badly treated that it had made them nervous or snappy. There was a Jack Russell Terrier named Lucy who had had cigarettes stubbed out on her, so that now she was so terrified she growled at everyone who came near.

"She's going to need a very special person to take her on," said Meg.

Then there was a poor German Shepherd who had been kept tied up in someone's backyard and never taken for walks and only fed on scraps. Meg said that when he first came to the shelter he was so weak he could hardly stand. Even now he was still a bit wobbly on his back legs. She said that he was another one who would need a special sort of person.

"He's as lovable as Mud, but he's frightened of his own shadow, poor boy. He'll need very careful handling."

She said that Mud was lucky because he had a happy temperament.

"In spite of all he's been through, he still trusts people."

I think it is terrible, what some human beings do to animals.

Mom always asked us, when we got home, how Mud was doing. I usually said, in reproachful tones, that he was "really miserable, shut up in a cage all by himself." But after Meg had told us about Mom crying I felt sort of sorry for her, so that day when she asked I said that he was "cheering up a bit."

"I mean, it's still horrible for him but at least he has a happy temperament. Some of the poor dogs are *really* unhappy."

"Like Caesar," said Jilly. Caesar was the German Shepherd.

"Yes, and Lucy. Meg says it's going to be really difficult finding the right people for them. She thinks someone is bound to want Mud because of him being so lovable."

"Well, there you are, then!" said Mom.

She sounded relieved. I suppose she thought we were beginning to get over our passion, but it wasn't that at all. It was just that we felt sorry for her. Well, I did, because she was my mom and I couldn't bear the thought of her crying. I don't expect Jilly minded so much. I mean, I wouldn't particularly care if her mom cried. Other people's moms aren't the same as your own.

My mom wanted to know if we were going to visit Mud again tomorrow.

Jilly said, "Yes! We're going to see him every single day until he finds a home."

"Good," said Mom. "In that case, you can take him a little present." And she suddenly produced a big bag of leathery chews! "I got them when I went shopping. I thought you could take them with you and hand them out to all the dogs. Only you'll have to check with Meg first, of course. Make sure it's all right."

Next day when we set off for school, I was carrying not only my school bag full of books but a plastic bag containing the leathery chews and a big rubber ball, which Benjy had insisted that I was to take "for Dub." He said that he and Dub had played with it together in the garden and that Dub would like it "'Cod it'd mind him ob me."

It really cracked me up when Benjy said

that. I think it cracked Mom up a bit, too, because I saw her bottom lip start to quiver. It's funny about people crying; you don't expect your mom to do it. My mom didn't even cry when she and Dad were splitting up (not unless she did it in private). But here she was with her lip quivering over Mud! And I knew that she'd cried when she'd left him at the shelter. So maybe her heart wasn't made of granite, after all. Just ordinary stone.

"Though, if she'd really been thinking of Mud," I said to Jilly as we cycled out to the shelter that afternoon, "she'd have kept him in spite of him being big."

Whatever Mom said, he wasn't as big as all that.

"Maybe if she came to visit him," said Jilly, "if she saw how unhappy he was . . . maybe she might change her mind. Maybe . . ."

Jilly stopped. I knew what she was going to suggest. I'd been thinking of it, too.

"Maybe we should get her to come along."

"Yes, and bring Benjy."

Mom is always a softie where Benjy is concerned. I don't mean she spoils him, because she tells him off just the same as she does me if he's naughty, but she's, like, extra protective toward him. She gets really angry if anyone tries to suggest that he's foolish or anything, just because he can't hear too well. Like she goes positively crazy if people talk about him being deaf.

She snaps, "He's not deaf! He's just hard of hearing."

I think Mom's a bit oversensitive, to be honest, but I guess it's on account of his problems. He tends to get special treatment.

Please don't think that it bothers me, because it absolutely doesn't. I'm not in the least bit jealous. As a matter of fact, I tend to be quite protective toward Benjy myself. If anyone says anything against him, or tries making fun of him or anything, I'm down on them *zap!* Right away. But just because I stick up for him doesn't mean I won't take advantage if I think it's going to help me get around Mom!

"I'll see if she'll come with us on Saturday," I said.

"You could tell her that Benjy would like to

see all the animals."

"Yes, all the cats and the rabbits."

"And guinea pigs!" said Jilly. "Someone brought in some guinea pigs the other day."

"Benjy adores guinea pigs," I said.

They had some at the special school he used to go to. Benjy was always talking about them. He used to call them "the dinnee bit."

I made up my mind that I would tell him about Meg's "dinnee bit" and then get him to ask Mom. She wouldn't be able to say no if it were Benjy!

I felt happy when I had worked out this plan of action, almost as if Mud were going to come home with us that very same evening. How could even Mom resist him when she saw him drooping in his cage?

Jilly and I bicycled into the yard, left our bikes leaning against the shed, which Meg used as an office, and went racing off with our bag of goodies to see Mud.

And that was when we had this terrific shock: Mud's cage was empty! He wasn't there!

"Oh!" wailed Jilly. "You don't think something's happened to him?"

"Like what?" I said.

"Like he might have got the distemper thing or the wotsit virus!"

"Parvovirus." My stomach churned at the very thought. Meg had told us about parvo, about how a dog could seem well one day and be dead the next. She had told us how one woman she knew had gone to bed and left her dog in the kitchen, and when she came downstairs next morning she found that it had been sick and bad all night without her knowing, and it was too late to do anything. (Which is a good reason, if you ask me, for letting a dog sleep in your bedroom. At least that way you'd know if it was ill.)

"It really is a deadly disease," Meg had told us. "That's why it's so desperately important for all dogs to be vaccinated against it."

And why she'd given Mud his shots in case he hadn't been. It seemed all too likely that a creep who tried to drown his dog in a suitcase wouldn't bother to get him injected against parvo. But suppose he'd caught the virus *before* Meg had given him his shots?

"Quick!" I shrieked. "Let's go and find out!"

As we raced back to the office we met Meg on her way across the yard.

"Oh! Girls." Meg beamed at us. "Good news! Mud's found a home for himself."

She said that a woman had come to the shelter that morning looking for a dog. She had brought her little girl with her and the little girl had fallen in love with Mud on sight.

"They only live a short way away so I did a home visit there and then, and that was it . . . they've adopted him!"

Jilly and I were silent. Meg obviously expected us to be as thrilled as she was. We were immensely relieved, of course, that Mud hadn't gotten parvovirus, and truly happy that he'd been given a chance to make a home for himself. But it was still a shock. We'd thought we'd be given the chance to say a proper goodbye.

"I'm sorry I couldn't let you know," said Meg. "I did think of calling your mom, but I knew you'd be at school. And they wanted him so badly! The little girl was absolutely delighted."

I hated that little girl. I shouldn't have, but I

did. Mud was mine! Mine and Jilly's! I guess the truth was that I was jealous. Just as meanly and horridly as Geraldine Hooper. But this little girl had gotten my dog!

Jilly, in a funny cracked sort of voice, said, "Has he got a nice big garden?"

"Well, it's not terribly large, but they've assured me they're going to take him for lots of long walks."

"It's not the same as having a proper garden."

"It is a *proper* garden," said Meg gently.

"I just hope it hasn't got flower beds in it," said Jilly.

"I just hope they'll be kind to him," I said.

"They will! I know they will. It's always very hard," said Meg, "letting a dog go when you've become attached to it, but that's what it's all about . . . finding homes for them. You can't possibly keep them all, much as you might like to."

But we hadn't wanted to keep them all! Just Mud. Just our own darling Mud, that was all we asked.

Jilly heaved a quivering sigh. I held out

Mom's bag of leathery chews.

"We brought these for him," I said.

"Well, now . . . there are lots of our other dogs who wouldn't say no. Shall we go around and give them out?"

The only dog we weren't allowed to give one to was Lucy, in case she snapped.

"She's getting a lot better," said Meg, "aren't you, my precious? But she's got a long way to go."

Meg gave her one and we left her Benjy's ball, as well, because we felt so sorry for her. Her poor little body was covered in these dreadful marks where the cigarettes had been stubbed out. Caesar, the big shepherd, took a chew as gently as could be. Meg said that in general he was still frightened of strangers, but "not of you two. You obviously have a way about you."

I liked the thought that I had a way with dogs, and Jilly was so pleased, you could tell.

"Now that you're here," said Meg, "I suppose you wouldn't care to lend a hand?"

Of course we said that we would, and so she gave us each a brush and comb and sent us into a small enclosure, which opened off the main big one. There were six dogs in there, all wildly excited to see us. Meg said, "There you are! Take your pick. They're all friendly—and they could all do with a grooming."

I could see that Jilly was a bit nervous, being surrounded by so many dogs, but I didn't mind one little bit. I loved it! They all came pushing at us, eager for attention. One big fluffy one that I thought might have a bit of Old English Sheepdog in him actually jumped up and put his paws on my shoulders, and so I started with him and just worked my way through, and Jilly did the same, except that she started on the smallest and quietest, a tiny little black mongrel named Fairy.

It was almost 5:00 by the time we'd finished and we had to rush because of getting back.

"This is absolutely splendid!" said Meg. "I can't thank you enough!" She said that most dogs enjoy being groomed and especially dogs that are in a shelter. "It's the attention they crave more than anything. They feel so starved for affection, poor things." And then she said, "You know you're welcome here at any time.

Mud may have gone to a new home, but there are all these others who need love and attention while they're waiting to be adopted. So if ever you have a spare moment . . ."

We promised her that we would have lots of spare moments.

"Like probably tomorrow," said Jilly.

I desperately wanted to be silent on the way home and think of Mud, but Jilly was bubbling over with excitement. She had groomed all those dogs—she had been in the enclosure, *surrounded* by them! She couldn't stop talking about it.

"Did you see that funny little white one with the patch over his eye? He kept making these little noises"—Jilly demonstrated, grunting like a pig. "And that one with only three legs! Meg said he'd been run over. I didn't know a dog could manage on only three legs, did you? But he was actually jumping up at me. And that *teeny* little one—"

She went on and on. Normally I'd have joined in, but I was still trying to examine my feelings and see how I felt about Mud going to a new home. All I could think was "please let them be kind to him!"

". . . *snuffling* over me," said Jilly, "And then giving me his paw to hold. It was so funny! I think someone must have taught him to say how do you do."

I hadn't the heart to tell her to shut up; it wouldn't have been fair. I just let her carry on until in the end she ran out of steam and said, "Well, anyway, at least we brought a little joy into their lives."

"Yes," I said. "At least we did that."

And then we bicycled in silence for a bit and thoughts of Mud flooded over me and I came bursting out with it before I could stop myself: "I just hope they're kind to him!"

Of course Jilly knew at once that it was Mud I was thinking of.

"So do I!" she said.

"I couldn't bear the thought that people might be cruel to him again."

"Oh, *don't!*" cried Jilly. And then she edged up so that we could ride side by side, now that we had reached Honeypot Lane. It meant she wouldn't have to shout anymore. "I know it's not the same without Mud," she said, "but I do think we ought to keep going there, don't you? To the shelter. I mean, it's true what Meg said, about the others. Mud doesn't need us anymore, but they do."

Jilly had become a true dog person. I was really proud of her!

I said, "Yes, I think we ought to. I think from now on we should dedicate our lives to helping animals."

"In the name of Mud," said Jilly.

There and then we made a solemn pact: in the name of Mud . . .

Chapter 6

When we went to the shelter on Friday after school, Meg said that she'd like us to try taking Caesar for a walk.

"The same place you took Mud . . . just up the lane and into the field."

She said she thought that Caesar would go with us "as you have a way with you."

Jilly wanted to know if we should take the ball, but Meg said no, she thought just a nice gentle stroll around the field would be enough for him at the moment.

"He isn't up to full strength yet. His back legs are still rather weak."

Meg told us that some German Shepherds have trouble with their back legs. She said if you buy one from a breeder you have to be very careful to check that it's not "in the strain." She said it's a tragedy if their back legs go when they're still only seven or eight years old, which is what can happen sometimes.

"Some people buy special little carts, with a harness, which they strap onto the dogs to help them walk, but it's only a temporary solution. They have to be put down in the end. It really is heartbreaking. And it's all come about," said Meg, sounding rather angry, "because of greedy, grasping breeders! They over-breed these poor creatures and then they get these terrible defects."

Fortunately, she said that she didn't think Caesar had a defect. She thought with him it was just that he had been so badly treated and not given enough to eat.

"You should have seen him when he first came here . . . it was pitiful. He could hardly even crawl. Look at him now! He's doing so well. He really has a will to live. And I've a gentleman coming to see him tomorrow. I've already done a home visit and it would be absolutely perfect, so I'm keeping my fingers crossed. The poor lad's been here over two months. It's high time he had a home."

Caesar was incredibly sedate after Mud! Not that Mud was rough but he was *bouncy*. He was still a puppy, of course; Caesar was a grown dog. He padded along at our side as quiet as could be, every now and again looking up at us, as if to check that everything was all right. We assured him that it was. We said, "Good boy, Caesar! Good *boy!*" and his tail wagged, very slowly, in acknowledgment.

Jilly and I agreed that it gave us a feeling of deep satisfaction to know that we were doing something to help animals that had suffered.

"And it's all thanks to Mud," said Jilly.

"Yes," I said, and even now I couldn't suppress a sigh.

"Oh, look, I *know*," said Jilly. "I miss him, too!"

But she couldn't miss him as much as I did! She hadn't spent a whole night sleeping with him. I kept remembering the feel of his funny prickly whiskers against my cheek and his long furry front legs around my neck. And as he slept he made these little whiffling noises, all night through.

"We have to think of the others," urged Jilly.

I knew that she was right. And I *was* thinking of the others. I really was! That was the reason I had come here after school and was taking Caesar for a walk when I could have been doing—oh, all sorts of other things. But just because I was thinking of the others didn't stop me thinking about Mud, as well.

We arrived home at 5:00 as usual and promised to meet up again after lunch the next day. Because it was Saturday, we were going to spend all afternoon at the shelter, helping Meg with the animals.

Jilly went off to have her dinner and I went off to have mine, and afterward I settled down to watch my nightly soap opera, which Mom thinks is stupid and I suppose I agree with her in a way, but sometimes stupid things can be fun. Also, they can take your mind off other things.

I was still watching television when the phone rang, which is why I didn't immediately rush to answer it, as I usually do. (I like answering telephones. You never know who is going to be on the other end.)

Mom got up and went into the hall and I

heard her give our number, and then I *thought* I heard her say, "Oh, hello, Meg!" except that I couldn't be sure because just at that moment there was lots of noise from the show and it blocked out Mom's voice. But after she'd gotten off the phone she went straight out through the front door only to come back in again a few minutes later through the back one.

"What *are* you doing?" I said.

"Oh, nothing," said Mom. "Just having a look around."

"What for?" My show had finished by then and it was the 6:00 news. I don't much care for news. It's usually so boring.

"I thought I heard something," said Mom.

"Burglars?" I said hopefully. I figured if we could have burglars it would make Mom wish she'd let us keep Mud. (Better than a burglar alarm!) I suppose there were moments, if I am honest, when I still wanted her to feel guilty.

But Mom said it wasn't burglars, it wasn't anything. She'd been mistaken.

"So who was it on the phone?"

"Well, really!" said Mom. "Talk about nosey!"

"I thought I heard you say 'Hello, Meg.'"

"Oh, did you?" said Mom. "And maybe you've heard of the saying, curiosity killed the cat?"

"No. Why did it?"

"Because it asked too many questions, I should think!"

She obviously wasn't going to tell me, which I thought she would have done if it had really been Meg, so I forgot all about it and went off to play with Benjy for half an hour before the week's top 10 videos came on. (Another program Mom thinks is stupid!) She enjoys boring old stuff like documentaries, which I can't stand unless they're about animals.

After the top 10, I killed another hour watching MTV, but then I got tired of that and there wasn't much on—either a gardening program, a soppy comedy, or this crime show, which Mom doesn't let me watch very often, mainly because she likes the soppy comedy.

So it was while Mom was watching the soppy comedy that the phone rang again, and this time I went racing off to answer it, and I snatched up the receiver and said, "Hello?" before Mom could get there. It was Meg at the other end and she said, "Oh! Hello, it's Meg. Is that—" And then Mom went and took the receiver off me so I couldn't hear any more except what Mom was saying at her end, which went something like this:

"Really? Good! Thank heavens for that! Where did they—oh, right! Not so very far. Well, perhaps they'll have learned their lesson . . . yes. Absolutely! Anyway, thanks for letting me know."

Mom put the receiver down and I said, "So it *was* Meg!"

"Yes, it was," said Mom.

"Why didn't you tell me?"

"I didn't tell you because I didn't want you to be upset. When Meg called the first time it was to ask if by any chance Mud had turned up."

"*Mud?*" I cried.

"Yes. Apparently," said Mom, "he was out for a walk with his new owners and they lost him. So they called Meg and she called us. Just in case he'd found his way here. I didn't want you to be worried."

"But I'd have gone and looked for him! Why didn't you let me? He could have been out there! He could've—"

"He could have been," said Mom, "but he wasn't. He was quite close to home, and now they've found him again. So all is well. No cause for concern. Yes?"

She put a finger under my chin and tilted my head toward her. "Yes?"

"No!" I twisted my head away. "How could they go and lose him?"

"Well, it seems they took a chance and let him off the leash and he just—disappeared. Meg was rather annoyed because she did tell them not to."

I was silent when Mom said that. I'd like to have said how stupid and thoughtless Mud's new owners were—I mean, fancy letting him off the leash when they'd only just gotten him! Everyone knows that a dog has to get used to you and accept you as his people.

That's what I'd like to have said but of course I couldn't. After all, I'd done exactly the same thing myself.

"Clara, sweetheart, do cheer up!" said Mom. She put an arm around me and coaxed me back into the living room. "I know you're still mad at me about Mud. What can I do to make it up to you?"

"Nothing," I muttered. There wasn't anything she could do. There wasn't anything she could bribe me with. I didn't want sneakers or a stereo. I just wanted my dog back!

"Suppose . . ." Mom sat down on the sofa and pulled me down next to her. "Suppose I said we'd get a puppy right away? I was going to wait until the spring, but suppose we do it right now? How would that be? Imagine a little puppy . . . a little Cocker Spaniel. So tiny it could sit in the palm of your hand! You'd like that, wouldn't you? Wouldn't you, Clara?"

I humped a shoulder. "I s'pose so."

"Well, try to look a bit happy about it!" said Mom. "I'm offering you a puppy!"

And of course, puppies are always lovely. Nobody can resist a little bundle of fluff. But I just had this stubborn feeling that no puppy, however gorgeous, could ever make up for the loss of Mud.

"Oh, Clara, please!" begged Mom. "Don't be like that!"

"Like what?" I mumbled.

"Resentful."

I said, "I'm not resentful, but—"

"Stop!" Mom suddenly jumped up. She whirled across the room and grabbed the local paper off the table. "Let's look in the pets columns! See what we can find."

We looked all through them. We found lots of Labradors for sale, and German Shepherds, and Dobermans. We even found something called a Shih Tzu (pronounced Shit Soo, which sounds rather rude to me. I'd almost have liked one just so I could tell people that that's what I had . . . a Shit Soo!) What we didn't find was one single Cocker Spaniel.

"On Monday I'll call the Kennel Club," said Mom. "Ask them for the names of some breeders."

In the meantime, she said, when we went into town tomorrow morning she would buy some dog magazines. There might be something in one of them.

"I am determined to get us a puppy!"

I tried to be enthusiastic, because Mom was doing her very best to make things up to me, but that night in bed I dreamed about Mud. I dreamed that he was curled up asleep on top of the comforter. I even heard his little whiffling sounds. It was so vivid that when I woke up I actually reached out to touch him—but of course he wasn't there. He was with his new owners now. He was their dog, not mine.

Next morning, we went into town. Jilly couldn't come with us, unfortunately. Her mom said she had been out too much lately and was to stay in and clean her bedroom, so Mom and Benjy and I drove in on our own, with Benjy sitting in front so he could get out quickly when he wanted to throw up. Benjy does a *lot* of throwing up. It's really very annoying. Every few minutes he's at it.

He yells, "Donna be dick!" And then, if Mom doesn't screech to a halt immediately, "Donna be dick *dow!*" At which point I hurl myself into the corner, just in case. Because when Benjy is sick, believe me, he is *sick.* And boy, he has a really good range!

"Why can't he take something for his stomach?" I grumbled, as we stopped for the third time. (I was feeling really grumpy.)

Mom said, "Stop picking on him. He'll grow out of it."

"In the meantime," I said, "the hedges are full of his puke."

"Clara, do you mind?" said Mom.

"Well, but it's so *boring*," I said.

Mom said that it was far worse for Benjy than it was for me and that I should learn to be a bit more tolerant. She said, "If it was a dog that was getting sick you wouldn't be so unkind."

Naturally, that made me think of Mud, and I became all woeful and sniffly and even grumpier than before.

As soon as we hit town Mom marched us into a bookshop and found a dog book and showed us a picture of a Cocker Spaniel.

"There!" she said. "What do you think?"

I studied it, grudgingly.

"It's eyes are all poppy," I said. "They look as if they're going to fall out."

It wasn't any use. I didn't want a Cocker Spaniel. I just wanted my own darling Mud!

On the way back to the car, after we'd done a whole load of shopping and were going to dump it, I saw this lady shaking a can. She was wearing a sash that said Animal Lovers, which immediately made me interested. Once I might just have walked on past, but now, because of Mud, my mind was full of animals almost every minute of the day.

So I rushed over and gave the lady 50 cents, and she smiled at me and said, "Thank you very much!" and stuck a yellow sticker on the front of my sweater.

It was a really nice sticker. It had a little picture of a cat and dog and around the edge it said We Love Animals. I thought that Jilly would like one, too.

"Do you think I could have one for my friend?" I said. "We are really into animals." And then I thought perhaps I was being a bit greedy, wanting two for the price of one, so I put another 20 cents in the can and said, "That's for my friend."

"That's very kind of you," said the lady, and she tore off another sticker with the backing paper still stuck on to it so that I could keep it safe for Jilly.

"What do Animal Lovers actually do?" I asked.

"We fight for animals," said the lady. "All animals, everywhere. We speak up for them."

I would have loved to stay and ask her more, but Mom was drooping under the weight of all the shopping and was desperate for a coffee and so on that occasion I wasn't able to. (I did later! But that is another story.) For the moment, I had to be content with just having the stickers.

We dumped the shopping in the car, and made our way to a sandwich shop so that Mom could have her coffee and take Benjy to the toilet, because Benjy *always* has to go to the toilet. And while she was taking him who should come up to me but Geraldine Hooper and her crummy friend, Puffin Portinari. (Don't ask *me* why she's called Puffin. Maybe because she's got this huge beaky nose and no neck.) So Geraldine looked at my We Love Animals sticker and sniffed, and went, "Oh! We just *lurve* animals," in a silly, sickly, simpering voice.

I just looked at her, very cold and serious, to show her that I was not amused.

So then she tossed her head and said, "Don't say you've gone and given *money* to them!"

I said, "No, I've given them five purple pumpkins," which for some reason struck me as being rather smart (though now I find it utterly pathetic and wish I could have thought of something cleverer).

Geraldine cackled and said, "Be better if you *had*."

And Puffin said, "*Yeah*," and nodded her stupid head without any neck.

So I said, "Why? What's your problem?" Geraldine told me that you shouldn't give money to animal charities because it's taking money away from the things that matter, such as cancer research, such as AIDS, such as, for example, *people.*

Puffin nodded again and said, "*Yeah.*"

"It means you care more about animals than human beings," said Geraldine, and I felt like smashing her face in, only Mom and Benjy came back just then so I couldn't, which was probably just as well. But they made me so mad!

"Were those two of your school friends?" asked Mom, trying to take a motherly interest.

I said, "No. They're a couple of total *dweebs*."

I made a mental note to tell Jilly. There are a lot of things I have to tell Jilly about. I just hope I can remember them all!

Chapter 7

On the way to the shelter that afternoon I gave Jilly her We Love Animals sticker. She thought it was absolutely super. I knew she would!

I told her about bumping into the idiotic dweebs and what Geraldine had said about us caring more for animals than for people. We discussed it as we bicycled along and decided that it simply wasn't true. We *did* care about people, but we cared about animals as well.

"Someone's got to help them," said Jilly.

"It's what the Animal Lovers do," I said. "They fight for animals."

"I think we should be Animal Lovers," said Jilly. "I think we should fight for animals."

And so we took a sacred, solemn oath: We would wear our yellow stickers and be Animal

Lovers and fight for "animals everywhere."

"And we won't take any notice of the idiotic dweebs."

We agreed that the dweebs were the sort of people who would deliberately crunch snails underfoot and chop worms in half.

"And throw dogs away in suitcases," said Jilly.

That, of course, reminded me of Mud, and how his new owners had gone and lost him and then found him again, so I told Jilly about that, as well. She said that she was really glad she hadn't known about it at the time because it would have really worried her. I said that Mom hadn't told me until it was all over.

"She didn't want me to be upset."

But I *was* upset. I kept thinking of Mud in his new home and worrying about how he was getting along. Whether he was happy, how he was being treated.

"I just hope they weren't mad at him!"

I couldn't bear to think of anyone yelling at him or hitting him.

"If he'd come home," said Jilly, "do you think your mom would have let us keep him?"

I said, "No! She's going to get a Cocker Spaniel!"

There was a silence, then Jilly heaved a sigh.

"If we can't have Mud, I suppose a Cocker Spaniel would be better than nothing. At least we'd be able to take it for walks."

And we would love it, of course, because as I had said to Mom, a dog is a dog. They are all beautiful. But I knew in my heart that nothing could ever take the place of our own special darling Mud. I would miss him forever!

Meg had a beaming smile when we arrived at the shelter because the nice man who had been coming to look at Caesar had immediately decided that he had to have him, and Caesar had gone off with him as happily as could be, so that was one piece of good news.

Another piece of good news was that a lady had called wanting a small terrier and had been so moved when she heard about poor Lucy and her cigarette burns that she had wanted to take her there and then.

"She's coming at 5:00," said Meg. "It would

be really wonderful if I could find a home for Lucy!"

"It is such a comfort," said Jilly, "to know that there *are* nice people in the world."

"Yes, like you and Clara," said Meg. "Now, what do you want to do this afternoon?"

"We could always take Lucy out," I said. I was still feeling upset about Mud and what had happened last night and I really wanted a challenge.

"Mmm . . ." Meg sounded doubtful. "I'm not sure that she'd go with you."

"We could try," I said.

I could see that Jilly was hesitating, because of Lucy still being liable to snap, but we couldn't just concentrate on the sweet-natured dogs, like Caesar. Not if we were really serious about helping animals. After all, it wasn't Lucy's fault that she'd been made nervous and bad-tempered; it was some creep of a human being who had done it to her. She deserved to be loved just as much as the others. And anyway, it would be a *test*.

Lucy wasn't too happy when Meg first brought her out and handed the leash to me.

She dug her little short legs in and wouldn't move. Meg said, "Don't drag her," but I wasn't going to. I coaxed her, instead. I said, "Come on, Lucy! Good girl! There's a good girl . . . come on! Good girl!" And after a few minutes she seemed to decide that perhaps Jilly and I were OK. Maybe it was because we weren't smoking cigarettes, or maybe it was because we weren't men. It was a man, Meg said, who had done the terrible things to her. She didn't think that Lucy would ever trust a man again.

By the end of the walk, she trusted Jilly and me! Meg had warned us not to try patting her, just in case she snapped, but when we got back she let us feed her with dog biscuits and even wagged her stumpy tail at us. (The reason her tail was stumpy was that it had been cropped. Meg said she didn't believe in cropping dogs' tails and neither do I. I think it is cruel and only done for effect.)

It is really *so* rewarding when you make a poor little dog like Lucy feel happy again.

On the way home, Jilly and I were discussing it when Jilly suddenly said, "You know what?"

I said, "What?"

"You know your mom wants to get a Cocker Spaniel?"

I said, "Yes."

"Well," said Jilly, "I don't think she ought to."

"Why not?" I said.

"Because I think she ought to go to the shelter and rescue one. I don't think," said Jilly, "that people ought to go to breeders. You heard what Meg said about them yesterday . . . greedy and grasping and over-breeding."

"They're not all like that," I said. I knew this because where we lived in New York there was a woman who bred toy poodles. Her house was full of them! She loved them to pieces. (Dad used to make fun of her because she used to talk to them in baby talk, but so what? It wasn't doing anyone any harm.)

"Some of them do it because they just love dogs," I said.

"I think if you *really* love dogs you should rescue them," said Jilly. "I think your mom needs working on."

It was so amazing! Just one week ago

she didn't know the first thing about dogs, and here she was, lecturing me! She was quite right, of course, but I did rather resent that about Mom.

"What about yours?" I said.

"We can work on mine later," said Jilly.

"Yours needs a *lot* of work."

Jilly admitted that she did. "That's why we ought to start on yours . . . she's already halfway there."

"It's no good thinking she'd adopt Lucy," I said. "She'd be scared in case she went and snapped at Benjy."

"No, but there are lots of others," urged Jilly.

"That's true," I said.

"So shall we speak to her? Before she goes and gets a Cocker Spaniel? I really think we ought to," said Jilly. "I mean, it's what it's all about, fighting for animals. I mean, we did take an *oath*. And just because it's your mom—"

Heavens! Jilly does go on.

"All right," I said. "I'll do it when I get in."

I knew I had to pick the right moment, and that the right moment definitely wasn't dinner time with Benjy messing his food around and whining that he wanted pizza, and Mom (for once) losing patience with him and asking why hadn't he thought of that earlier, when we were shopping?

"Cod I didn' ding ob it!" said Benjy. And then he looked at me and said, "Where'd Dub?" and banged his knife and fork on the table and said, "I wan' Dub! Why can' I hab Dub?"

I don't know what made him suddenly come out with that. Probably it was because he was mad at Mom for trying to make him eat something he didn't want to eat, and he thought that would be a way to get at her.

It was! Mom said, "Oh, for heaven's sake! Not again! Just go on and eat your food."

Definitely not a good moment for asking her about dogs.

I left it until later, when Benjy was in bed and Mom and I were alone together, and could have a more grown-up type of conversation. I started by asking Mom if she'd managed to find a Cocker Spaniel. Mom said, "No, I'm afraid I haven't. There don't seem to be any around. Of course, I suppose we could always have some other kind of dog. It doesn't *have* to

106

be a Cocker Spaniel."

That was when I seized my opportunity. I rushed in, just like Jilly had. I gave her all the arguments, all about the greedy, grasping breeders and the German Shepherds with their weak hind legs and little dogs like Lucy having their poor tails cut off. And then I reminded her of all the sad, unloved animals in Meg's shelter just waiting for someone to come along and give them a home, and how some of them had been mistreated, and some had been thrown out, and some had belonged to people that had died. And at the end of it all, Mom clapped her hands over her ears and begged, "Stop it, stop it, for goodness' sake! You've made your point. You've made me feel thoroughly guilty!"

"I didn't mean to do that," I said. Not quite truthfully, I have to admit.

"Oh, no?" said Mom. "Clara, you are a manipulator!"

"I just thought, if we can't have Mud—if we *really* can't have Mud—we could at least go and rescue another animal."

Mom threw up her hands. "All right! You win. When you go there tomorrow you can ask

Meg if she's got a suitable dog for us. And when I say suitable, Clara, I mean suitable. I don't mean dogs that weigh half a ton and come up as high as my shoulder. I mean something *small*."

I nodded. "Meg has lots of small dogs," I said. Though as a matter of fact she had lots more big ones. She had already told us that small ones were far easier to find homes for. Not so many people want the big ones because they are scared they will cost too much to feed; or else, like Mom, they say they haven't got room. And so it's the big ones that tend to get left. But I didn't want to get Mom angry.

"I'll ask Meg," I said.

"Right," said Mom. "You find something small—and reasonably docile—and we'll think about it."

"If Meg says we can bring one home for you to see, can we do it?"

"So long as I'm allowed to say no if I don't think it's right."

"Oh, well, of *course*," I said. "Obviously!"

Jilly was so pleased when I told her the next day. She said, "This is our second act of animal rescue! We'll start on my mom after this."

I couldn't actually see that we were ever likely to get anywhere with Jilly's mom considering she goes crazy even if a pathetic starving bird just pecks a few berries off her rotten plants, but I didn't say so because I didn't want to upset Jilly. I can see it must be depressing having a mother who is so totally hostile to all forms of animal life.

We spent the rest of the ride out to the shelter discussing which dogs Mom might consider suitable. When it actually came to it, there weren't really all that many.

"Sam is lovely, but I suppose he's a bit too big."

"And Rosa."

Sam was part Boxer and Rosa was a cross Collie-Labrador. We sighed. They were both far too big.

"There's always Fairy. She's small."

"But she's 14! I don't know whether Mom would want a dog that's that old."

We sighed for the second time.

"People ought to rescue old dogs," said Jilly.

"Tell that to your mom!" I said.

"Well, anyway, Meg says she's going to let Fairy be an indoor dog from now on. She says she's too old to be kept in the kennels."

"What about Biscuit?" I said. Biscuit was the tiny little brown and white mongrel with only three legs. Meg reckoned he was half Yorkshire Terrier and half Corgi. "Mom couldn't say he was too big!"

"No, but he's already been brought back once because people said he was destructive. Do you think your mom would take a destructive dog?"

We sighed yet again.

"Honestly," said Jilly, "if it were me I'd just take whichever one was most in need of a home."

"I'd take them all," I said.

"Oh, well, yes, so would I," said Jilly.

Yet we couldn't even find one that Mom would think suitable!

"Perhaps more will have come in," I said.

More dogs *had* come in. We saw them in their kennels as we entered the yard. There were four of them. Two were rather large, one was quite tiny, and one was . . .

Chapter 8

"*Mud!*"

He was slumped on the floor of his cage, his head between his paws.

"Oh, Mud!" I cried.

We ran toward him, but he was too miserable even to respond to the sound of our voices. It wasn't until we reached his cage and he actually saw us that he came to life. He was up on his feet in an instant, hurling himself at the wire mesh, screaming and yelping in his frenzy to get at us.

"Oh, *Mud*," I said.

"Clara! Jilly!" Meg was hurrying toward us across the yard. "You've found him!"

"What happened?" asked Jilly. "Why is he back here?"

"They brought him in this morning, the poor

boy! And it's all my fault!"

For an awful moment I thought she was going to tell us something terrible, such as, for instance, that Mud's shots had been given to him too late and he had caught the dreaded parvo. Not that that would have been Meg's fault, but the whole of my insides were in such a whirl that I couldn't even think straight. All I knew was that Mud was back!

"They said they couldn't keep him. They said he was too much for them. I expect your mom told you, Clara, that they lost him when they took him for a walk? They said he just wouldn't respond when they called to him."

"He hadn't had time to learn his name!" Jilly said it indignantly.

"It wasn't that. I mean, they ought not to have let him off the leash so soon, but that wasn't what the problem was. It was something I should have discovered while he was at the shelter. Let me show you."

All this time, poor old Mud was trying his hardest to get at us, standing on his hind legs and clutching at the mesh with his front paws.

"Watch this," said Meg.

She disappeared behind the row of kennels. Jilly and I stayed where we were, pushing our fingers through the mesh, wiggling them at Mud and making soothing sounds. His tail was going in circles, and he kept nibbling at our fingertips, incredibly gently.

"Watch!" called Meg.

She had come into his kennel, through a door at the back. She was holding a big metal tray and a wooden spoon. Suddenly, she sent the spoon crashing into the tray. It made a tremendous noise, like a giant cymbal thundering around the yard. All the other dogs started barking and running around excitedly—except Mud. He just went on clutching at the mesh and nibbling our fingers as if the terrific noise had never happened.

Meg moved closer and whacked the tray a second time. She was right behind Mud now, but he still didn't react.

"You see?" said Meg. "The poor boy is totally deaf!"

"Hard of hearing," I muttered, just out of habit, really.

"Call it what you like," said Meg. "The fact

is, he can't hear a single thing."

"And that's why they brought him back?" Jilly sounded shocked. "Just because he can't hear?"

"They felt they couldn't cope. Some people are like that. Although in fact," said Meg, "most dogs learn to manage quite well. On the other hand, it *is* a handicap and I ought to have discovered it sooner. He's such a bright boy that no one noticed."

"We didn't notice," said Jilly, "did we?"

"No, we didn't," I said. But I said it a bit vaguely because my brain was racing, working overtime.

"And if anyone should have noticed, we should," said Jilly, "because of Benjy."

"Of course," said Meg. "Clara's little brother! So you know all about it."

"Well, Clara does," said Jilly.

Meg was standing with her arm around Mud, stroking his chest.

"He must have been born this way. It's so sad. It happens with some dogs; nobody seems to know why."

"Does that mean that no one will want

him?" said Jilly.

"It will certainly make it a lot more difficult. People get frightened at the thought of a dog with a handicap."

"So he could be here for weeks?"

"I'm afraid he could. But at least he'll have you and Clara to visit him and take him for walks."

I suddenly switched into action.

"Could we take him for one now?" I said.

"By all means. That would be wonderful! Just what's needed to cheer the poor boy up."

"Could we take him for a really long one? Not just into the field, but a *long* one?"

"So long as you don't let him off the leash. I can think of nothing he'd like better!"

So Jilly and I set off with Mud, me holding the leash and Jilly talking a mile a minute in my ear.

"That's why he didn't come back when we called him, that first day. He couldn't hear us! And that's why he never knows when we've come to visit him until we're right in front of him and he can see us. *And* why your mom thought he was stupid! Do you remember? She asked him if he was crazy. She said she didn't think he was very bright. Which is *such* a mean thing to say! 'Cause he's as bright as bright can be. And now nobody's going to want him, just because he can't hear, and it's so rotten, and— *Clara!*"

She caught at my arm. "Where are we going?"

"We're taking him home," I said.

"Taking him *home?*"

"To see Mom."

There was a pause. A rather startled sort of pause. Mud forged ahead on the end of his leash, pulling me along with him, so that Jilly had to trot to keep up.

"Your mom said she wanted something small!"

"Yes, I know."

"*And* she wanted a female."

"Not necessarily."

"That's what she said once."

"She didn't say it yesterday. She just said something small and docile."

"But Mud isn't either of those things!"

"No, but he's deaf," I said.

We went in through the back yard. Benjy

116

was out there on his own, floating his fleet of toy ships across his wading pool. When he saw Mud he yelled "*Dub!*" and came running over.

Mud was so pleased to see him! He jumped up with a joyous bark, his front paws going like windmills.

"Benjy, we've discovered something," I said. "Mud's like you . . . he can't hear properly. He's deaf."

"Deb dod!"

"That's right," I said. "Deaf dog."

Benjy was delighted. We left him in the yard, hugging Mud and chanting, "*Baw*, Dub, *baw*, Dub! Deb dod!" while we went off to find Mom.

Jilly was a bit nervous. "Your mom is going to be furious," she said.

I knew that she'd have gone rushing back out into the garden and left me to do battle all by myself, but I sternly reminded her that we had sworn to fight for animals and she couldn't just back out the minute things started to get tough.

"Oh, all right," sighed Jilly, and she trailed along behind me into the kitchen, doing her best to be invisible.

Mom was in the living room, with her feet up. She was surprised to see me and Jilly.

"Back so soon?" she said.

"We've . . . um . . . got something to show you," I said.

"A dog?" Mom sat up. "I hope it's small! And docile."

Jilly swallowed. I saw her Adam's apple bob up and down.

"It's . . . um—"

"It's what?"

"It's Mud," I said.

"*Mud?*" Mom's eyebrows knitted themselves together in a great big storm cloud of a frown. "Clara," she said, "I warned you! I—"

"They brought him back, Mom!"

"They didn't want him—"

"They said they couldn't cope—"

"He was so unhappy!"

"That is no reason," snapped Mom, "for bringing him back here! You had absolutely no right! You can take him straight back again. And this time—"

"But he's deaf, Mom!"

There was a pause.

"What's that got to do with it?" said Mom.

"It's why they didn't want him."

"And why his creep of a first owner tried to drown him, I bet!"

"Yes, because he probably thought Mud was brain damaged."

There was another pause.

"It's what people used to think about Benjy," I said. "They used to think he was brain damaged, just because he couldn't hear properly."

Mom bit her lip. "Clara, you're trying to manipulate me," she said.

"But it's so unfair, Mom! Just because he's handicapped."

"Meg said he could be in the kennels for *weeks*."

"Just fading away—"

"And pining away—"

"All because he's deaf!"

Mom raised her hands and let them fall again.

"So where is he now?" she asked.

"He's out in the yard, with Benjy. Benjy was

so happy to see him."

"Benjy really loves him," said Jilly.

"Thank you, Jilly," said Mom. "One manipulator is quite enough. Don't you start."

Jilly shot me a scared glance. But it was all right: My mom isn't like hers.

"I will not be dictated to," said my mom.

She stalked through to the kitchen and out the back door, followed by Jilly and me. There in the yard, Benjy was busy trying to hook his hearing aid over one of Mud's ears.

"Benjy!" cried Mom. She ran over to him. "What are you doing?"

Benjy looked up and beamed. "Deb dod," he said. "Dub deb!"

Mom smiled weakly.

"I jare my eenin aid."

"Darling," said Mom. She spoke slowly, so that Benjy could lip-read. He's very good at that. "You cannot share your hearing aid with a dog."

Benjy's face fell. "Bud 'e'd deb!"

"I know he is, sweetheart. But dogs can't wear hearing aids. We'll just have to teach him sign language, instead."

Jilly's eyes flickered at me.

"*Mom!*" I said.

"Don't you come Mom-ing me!" said Mom. "That was out-and-out blackmail."

"Oh, but Mrs. Carter," gushed Jilly, "it wasn't meant to be."

"Yes, it was," said Mom. "You should be ashamed of yourselves! You'd better go and call Meg before I start having second thoughts."

Jilly and I zoomed back indoors to dial the number. We left Benjy in the yard with Mud. Benjy had hooked his hearing aid back on and was trying to teach Mud some elementary sign language.

"*Did.*" He jabbed his hand toward the ground. "Did dowd! Dub did *dowd.*"

I wouldn't say that Mud was taking no notice, exactly, but he did seem more interested in the wading pool and the fleet of boats.

Meg was busy the first time we tried her. The line to the shelter is always busy. Jilly signaled frantically at me. She was terrified that Mom would change her mind before she could commit herself.

121

"I'll keep trying," I whispered.

"Yes, you do that," said Mom, throwing Jilly into total confusion. Mom wasn't supposed to have heard! "And while we're waiting, let's all try to think of a more sensible name . . . I can't have a dog named Mud!"

"But he knows that name," I said.

"Clara, how can he know it when he can't hear?"

"He can lip-read," I said.

"So he can learn to lip-read something else. Something a bit more dignified. Horace or . . . Humphrey or . . . "

At that moment, the back door burst open and Mud came galloping in. He was wild-eyed, and being pursued by Benjy. In his jaws he was holding one of Benjy's boats. He was soaking wet and his feet were covered in—mud!

I flew to the kitchen window—the wading pool had been overturned and water was everywhere.

Mud raced into the hall, followed by Mom and Benjy. Jilly and I raced after them.

We all tore up the stairs in a line: Benjy, Mom, Jilly, and me, with Mud in the lead.

Mud's tail was stuck up straight, like a flag. He thought it was a fine game!

Straight into Mom's bedroom he raced. Wallop! Bang into the center of Mom's lovely pink comforter. Great splatty paw prints all over . . .

Jilly looked at me, and I looked at Jilly. My heart sank. "Oh, Mud!" I thought. "You've gone and ruined everything!"

There was a long, long, *very* long silence.

"Deb dod," said Benjy hopefully.

"He didn't mean it, Mom!"

"He couldn't help it!"

"He's only a dog!"

"Right." Mom took a deep breath. "You!" she pointed a finger at me. "Take that comforter off and put it in the washing machine. And you," she pointed at a cringing Jilly, "take that animal downstairs and get him cleaned up."

"M-Mom," I quavered.

"*Please*," begged Jilly.

"Take him," said Mom.

With tears in her eyes, Jilly jerked Mud off the bed and led him to the door.

"I was obviously wrong," said Mom. "It looks as if Mud is the right name for him after all." She put her hands on her hips and stuck her face close to Mud's. "Muddy Four Paws! And I've been blackmailed into keeping you!"

That was when I knew that it was going to be all right. Mud was ours! He was here to stay.